FOR MY DAD, WHO INTRODUCED ME TO MY FIRST PUFFER

Published by Roaring Brook Press
Roaring Brook Press is a division of Holtzbrinck Publishing Holdings Limited Partnership
120 Broadway, New York, NY 10271 • mackids.com

Library of Congress Cataloging-in-Publication Data is available.
ISBN 978-1-250-79699-8

Our books may be purchased in bulk for promotional, educational, or business use.
Please contact your local bookseller or the Macmillan Corporate and Premium Sales Department
at (800) 221-7945 ext. 5442 or by email at MacmillanSpecialMarkets@macmillan.com.

First edition, 2022 • Book design by Cindy De la Cruz
Printed in China by Hung Hing Off-set Printing Co. Ltd., Heshan City, Guangdong Province

ABOUT THIS BOOK
The illustrations for this book were created digitally using an iPad and Procreate. This book was edited by Mekisha Telfer and Connie Hsu and designed by Cindy De la Cruz with art direction by Sharismar Rodriguez. The production was supervised by John Nora, and the production editor was Avia Perez. The text was set in Melvin Sans, and the display type is handlettered.

1 3 5 7 9 10 8 6 4 2

HOW TO HUG A PUFFERFISH

ELLIE PETERSON

ROARING BROOK PRESS
NEW YORK

So you want to hug a pufferfish.

Who could blame you?
Those big ol' bubble eyes.

That gap-toothed grin.

The spotty skin, like moldy bread with mustard.

Could anything be cuter?

There are so many reasons to give Pufferfish a hug!

It could be that Pufferfish has just come back from a long trip.

Kelp Forest

Maybe Pufferfish has just won an award
and you want to say congratulations.

Or maybe Pufferfish is your very best friend and you really want to show you care.

There's only one teeny tiny thing to consider.

Never fear! Pufferfish might welcome a hug
from you, under the right conditions.
First, Pufferfish doesn't like surprises.

Loud sounds can startle Pufferfish.

Don't tickle or poke Pufferfish in place of a hug.

And if things go badly,

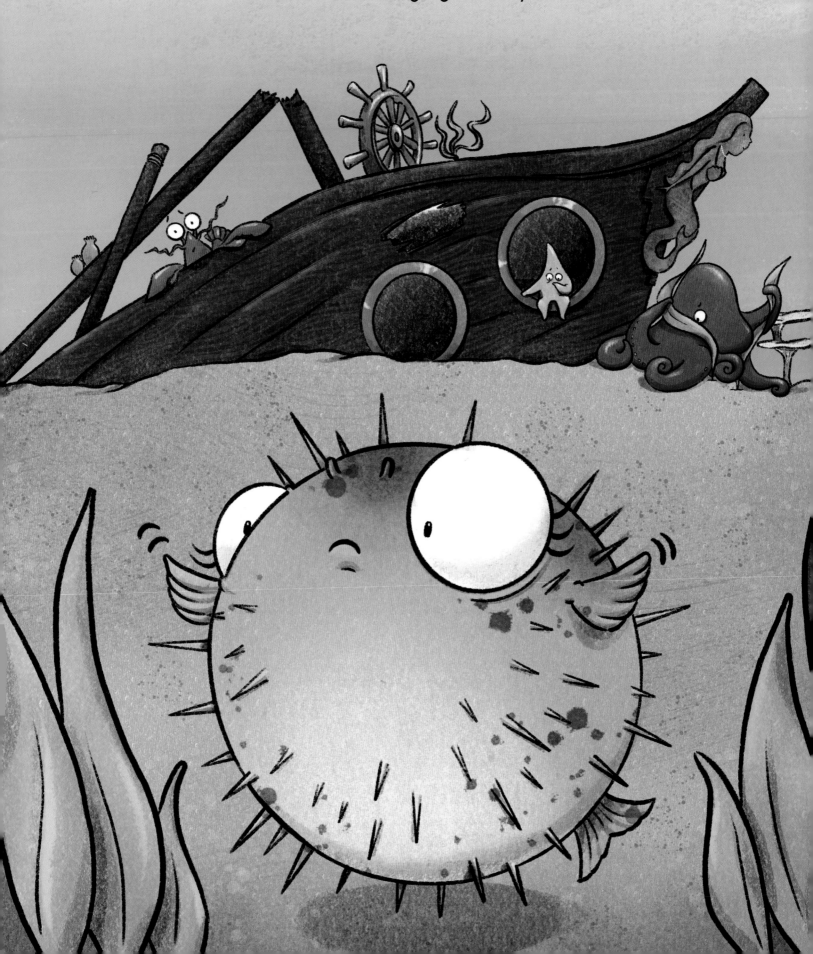

give Pufferfish some time to depuff before trying again.

Even if you love hugs, Pufferfish might prefer something different.

Pufferfish would like to see you coming.

Pufferfish would like to
be asked for a hug first.

Pufferfish would like your hug to be slow and gentle.

Pufferfish might even
prefer a high tail

or fin-shake instead.

And you never know.
Pufferfish might show
you a different way to say
I love you.

Now if you want to hug a sea urchin . . .
that's a whole other story.